# Born in the Breezes

## THE SEAFARING LIFE OF
## JOSHUA SLOCUM

# Born in the Breezes

## THE SEAFARING LIFE OF JOSHUA SLOCUM

by *Kathryn Lasky*

illustrated by *Walter Lyon Krudop*

ORCHARD BOOKS / NEW YORK

*An Imprint of Scholastic Inc.*

ACKNOWLEDGMENT

The author and illustrator would like to thank Andrew W. German, research fellow for

America and the Sea Exhibitions at Mystic Seaport, for his helpful suggestions

regarding the text and illustrations of this book.

10 9 8 7 6 5 4 3 2 1    01 02 03 04 05

Printed in Mexico   49

First edition, November 2001

Book design by Mina Greenstein

The text of this book is set in 14 point Scotch Roman.

The illustrations are oil paintings.

Library of Congress cataloging-in-publication data is available upon request.

ISBN 0-439-29305-7        LC 00-66565

To C.G.K., a seafaring man—K.L.

To Carol—W.L.K.

# Born in the Breezes

*I was born in the breezes, and I had studied
the sea as perhaps few men have studied it,
neglecting all else.*

——Joshua Slocum, *Sailing Around the World*

IN THE YEAR 1854, in the busy fishing town of Westport on Brier Island, Nova Scotia, a boy named Joshua sat hunched on a bench. He was pegging fishermen's boots in his father's boot shop. And he was bored.

The breeze from the sea blew in. He loved the smell of the salt air. He loved the slap of the waves. But he hated the stink of the vats where the leather soaked. He hated the monotonous sound of his hammer tapping in the pegs. Still, his father forced him to work in the boot shop.

Outside the shop the harbor was crammed with ships: coastal schooners; stately brigantines; fast, sleek sloops; and every kind of fishing vessel, from small lobster smacks to Grand Banks fishing schooners. Joshua longed to be on one of them.

Like so many young boys growing up in the Maritime Provinces of Canada, Joshua was drawn to the sea. For it was at sea that boys and men were tested. It was at sea that they found out for sure how brave they were, if they could walk across a rolling deck, if they could climb high into the rigging to change sail in a storm. It was at sea that one learned to steer a ship across a vast ocean by the position of the stars in the sky. Joshua wanted to be on a sailing ship with the smell of tar and salt and a slashing gale in his face.

When Joshua wasn't pegging boots, he loved to build models of the ships he saw in the harbor. Starting with a discarded hunk of wood and only a penknife, he could capture the sea-kindly lines of almost any vessel. He shaped the spars and sewed the sails and sanded, varnished, and finished these small ships until they glistened.

One day, just as he was getting ready to paint the name on one of his best creations, his father burst through the doorway. He picked up the model and smashed it to smithereens. He was outraged that his son was wasting his time with toy boats instead of helping with the family's livelihood.

Joshua's ship model was in splinters, but not his dreams. He decided to run away to sea. He was fourteen years old. The only job he could get was as cook on a fishing schooner. But cooking belowdecks with pots flying through the air and hot cauldrons of fish-head stews to stir was not what young Joshua had imagined. He was never once asked to climb the rigging or to steer by the stars. He returned home.

Finally at sixteen, when his mother died, Joshua left for good. He set sail on a ship bound for Dublin. From Ireland he sailed to China, from China to Australia.

Many men and boys who went to sea in those days had little learning. Many were rough and brutal. Some were criminals. Joshua, however, was different; he had a real love of learning. In his spare time he read all he could about the science of celestial navigation and practiced with the sextant, the instrument used for locating a ship's position on the sea by measuring the angles between the stars and the horizon. The officers of the ship noticed, and by the time Joshua was eighteen, he had been promoted from common sailor to second mate. By the time he was twenty-five, he had become Captain Joshua Slocum.

# A Rare and Courageous Wife

*Her flashing yellow-gold eyes . . . had the steady gaze of an eagle. . . .*
*It was a rarely courageous wife who accompanied her husband on*
*more than one voyage. But Virginia for the rest of her life sailed*
*wherever Captain Joshua went.*

—WALTER MAGNES TELLER, *The Voyages of Joshua Slocum*

*I*T WAS TWO YEARS LATER IN 1870, on a voyage to
Australia, that Joshua met the love of his life, Virginia Walker. Virginia
had been born in the United States. Her family had gone west to
California for the gold rush in 1849 and then continued farther west,
across the Pacific to Australia. Virginia was as tough as she was pretty.
She claimed to have American Indian blood. She was an expert horse-
back rider and a crack shot with a rifle. She also loved fishing. Joshua
and Virginia were both adventurers. They recognized this immediately
in each other.

Their marriage would be different, starting with the wedding. No long ceremony, fancy clothes, and big party for Virginia and Joshua. They dashed into a church in their street clothes and were married within a matter of minutes. Virginia kissed her mother and father good-bye, and then the young couple boarded Joshua's ship just in time to catch a favorable breeze and sail away.

It was their honeymoon. Joshua had been hired to captain a fishing vessel, so with a crew of foulmouthed sailors they headed for the salmon-fishing grounds in the northern Pacific near Alaska. The waters teemed with giant king salmon, fur seals, and birds.

Although she had not sailed much before, Virginia took to this new life instantly. She learned the mathematics of navigation and how to steer the ship. She could stitch a sail and gut a fish as expertly as anyone.

In Cook Inlet, Alaska, where they made camp, the fishing was good. With the holds full of salmon, they were about to head for San Francisco when a gale struck. Their ship was wrecked on a sandbar. But Slocum, through his ingenuity, managed to save both his bride and the fish cargo. He sent Virginia on ahead in a smaller ship. Then he built a whaleboat to carry himself and his crew, and used some smaller craft that had been aboard the wrecked ship to transport his catch. His bride and all the salmon were eventually delivered safely to San Francisco.

Neither fierce gales, shipwrecks, nor cursing sailors had dimmed Virginia's love of the sea. So in 1871 Joshua and Virginia sailed to Honolulu on board a new command, the *Constitution*.

# Shark Fishing
## and
## Star Math

*When a* Tribune *reporter visited the ship, Mrs. Slocum sat busily engaged with her little girl at needlework. Her baby boy was fast asleep in his Chinese cradle. An older son was putting his room in order and a second son was sketching.*

——from an article in *The New York Tribune*, June 26, 1882,
describing the Slocums' family life aboard ship

*I*T WAS ON THE *CONSTITUTION* that the Slocums' first child was born. Another child soon followed, and then two arrived at once when Virginia gave birth to twins in a storm-laced sea off the Kamchatka Peninsula of Siberia. In those days, however, many children died quite young, whether they were born at sea or on land. The twins died in infancy. In all, Joshua and Virginia had four children who survived: three boys and one girl.

The children did not go to school but were taught at sea by Virginia. They studied reading, writing, arithmetic, drawing, and celestial navigation.

What better math lessons could there be than the real "word problems" of figuring out exactly where a ship was in the middle of the Indian Ocean or the Tasman Sea by calculating the position of the stars? All four children learned to sew, for ship sails were in need of constant repair. And the children spent many days on deck with their mother, an accomplished artist, drawing seabirds, dolphins, or the playful fur seals that swam around their ship in the northern Pacific.

Their favorite subject, however, was shark fishing. Virginia and the children took turns dangling a lure of tin cans trailing shiny bits of metal in the water to attract a shark. Standing with a .32 caliber pistol, as steady as a housewife at her kitchen sink, Virginia kept watch for the fin slicing through the water. When a shark came into range, she took aim and fired. She never needed more than one shot.

Joshua Slocum was commissioned to captain many different ships. On the family's voyages, there were people to meet and wonderful souvenirs to barter for. At one stop in some islands off Alaska, Virginia bought a collection of fossil fish more than a million years old from the native people and explained to her children the mysteries of vanished life-forms and ancient geological secrets of the earth.

In these same islands, one day their father climbed aboard from the ship's small boat, followed by one of the strangest creatures the children had ever seen, a person who seemed more animal than human. "He's an otter," the eldest son, Victor, whispered. But in fact, the man was a hunter of sea otters, and Joshua Slocum had agreed to give him passage to a nearby island. The man's weather-beaten face peered out from the fur fringe of his anorak's hood. Every single thing he owned, from his long rifle to his cooking utensils, was tied to him with string made from seal gut. The children stood silent and amazed.

# Poetry, Pirates, and Naked Sampan Men

*From the decks of stout ships in the worst gales I
had made calculations as to the size and sort
of ships safest for all weather and seas.*

—JOSHUA SLOCUM, *Sailing Around the World*

JOSHUA SLOCUM stood aboard his command, the handsome *Amethyst*, in Nagasaki Harbor, Japan. He was part owner of the ship and had delivered every kind of cargo from coal to timber to gunpowder. He blinked and inhaled sharply as he looked across the water. Could it be? He squinted again as the sampan man approached. The sampan men were native boatmen hired by foreign captains to run errands ashore. This one was stark naked! Joshua heard his children giggling madly as they hung over the rail to watch the sight.

"Put on some clothes!" the captain roared in a voice fit for a gale.

The family soon became used to naked sampan men, however, as they began two years of sailing to Nagasaki in the China timber trade.

The entrance to Nagasaki had a dramatic rock cliff on one side, with twisted and crooked dwarf pines jutting from it. Joshua Slocum loved poetry and had a favorite rhyme that he felt matched the cliff perfectly. He would recite this verse to his children as they entered Nagasaki Harbor.

> *There was an old man of Comer*
> *Who stood on one leg to read Homer.*
> *When he felt it grow stiff,*
> *He jumped over the cliff,*
> *And that ended the old man of Comer.*

But it was not all poetry and naked sampan men. There were real dangers in this part of the world.

Joshua Slocum had just entered the Yangtze River in China. His children were on the deck as a sampan man approached and offered his piloting services for navigating the river. Just behind his boat, Slocum noticed a Chinese junk, well armed and manned by an especially rough-looking crew. He was not comfortable with the situation, but by this time the pilot was aboard, telling him where to go to avoid the shoal water.

Within a few minutes Slocum was alarmed. Something was wrong! Slocum knew in a flash that they were heading for shallow water. And he also sensed that the sampan man was a pirate.

Quickly Joshua spun the wheel and avoided running his ship aground. He gave a sharp order to his crew, who dumped the pirate back into his sampan. The children stood peering over the rail as the junk sailed over to the man. It had all happened so fast. A pirate had been on board the *Amethyst*! So close they could have touched him!

# The Finest American Vessel Afloat

*This vessel is the clipper ship* Northern Light. *. . . . A visit to her deck suggests two sad and striking thoughts, one that American sailing ships are becoming obsolete and the other that so few American sailors can be found. She is commanded by Captain Joshua Slocum, who is one of the most popular commanders sailing out of this port.*

—*The New York Tribune,* June 26, 1882

ONE FINE DAY IN JUNE OF 1882, Joshua Slocum sailed the magnificent *Northern Light* into New York Harbor. So tall was the rigging that the upper masts had to be struck as the ship passed under the Brooklyn Bridge, which was just being built. The *Northern Light* was the largest and most beautiful ship Joshua Slocum had ever commanded. There was even a library with over five hundred books aboard.

From New York, Slocum was to take a cargo of petroleum to Japan. Joshua and Virginia sensed at once that their crew was a troublesome bunch. There was one fellow in particular who seemed to be angry and suspicious of all the ship's officers.

Before the *Northern Light* was out of the sight of land, there was a problem with the rudder, and they were forced to turn back to the nearest port. All the sailors had been paid in advance, and some of them now wanted to use the rudder problem as an excuse to end the voyage.

Suddenly the crew stood stock-still, refusing to raise the sails or do any work. They demanded to be taken ashore. When Slocum refused, they rushed the quarterdeck, armed with handspikes. In the fray the chief mate was stabbed to death. Virginia heard the ruckus from below and ran on deck gripping a pistol in each hand to cover her husband as he sent a signal for help. The mutiny ended, and its leader was taken off the ship.

The *Northern Light* continued. The crew, however, remained surly. The ship sailed on a southerly course through the latitudes called the Roaring Forties, near the bottom of the globe where the wind always howled. Christmas was celebrated that year, but the ship was still troubled by grumbling sailors. Victor, Slocum's eldest son, described the long trip as "voyaging with a volcano under the hatches." By Christmas of the following year, Slocum began to look for a new ship.

He soon found her, the *Aquidneck*. It was an unusual ship, with a piano bolted to the deck, along with livestock pens atop the deckhouse for chickens, pigs, and geese. Family and crew set sail with a cargo of flour bound for South America. Their first stop was in Pernambuco, where they moored near a reef outside the port. Virginia took the children ashore for picnics, and then, in a smaller boat, they explored the reef to observe the coral formations, the fish, and the life of the reef as part of their natural history lessons.

But by the time they left the Pernambuco port, Virginia had become very ill. Shortly after the ship anchored in the harbor of Buenos Aires, she died. There would, of course, be more voyages and other ships, but without Virginia, life at sea for Joshua and the children would never be the same.

# The Spray

*Nearly all our tall vessels had been cut down for coal barges, and*
*were being ignominiously towed by the nose from port to port,*
*while many worthy captains addressed themselves to Sailors'*
*Snug Harbor. . . . Mine was not the sort of life to make one long*
*to coil up one's ropes on land, the customs and the ways of which*
*I had almost forgotten.*

—JOSHUA SLOCUM, *Sailing Around the World*

*I*T WAS 1892, eight years since Virginia had died. By then the children had grown up, and the entire world had changed for Joshua Slocum. Gas, steam, and electricity were beginning to power everything. The first American gasoline buggy, or motorcar, was produced. Electric lighting was installed for the first time in the White House. Over 125,000 miles of railroad track had been laid, connecting far corners of the continent.

Electric trolleys were moving people through cities. The power of the steam turbine was being used more and more for ships. Wind as a power source was considered old-fashioned in the busy, new world of commerce and communication. The time of the great sailing ships was drawing to a close.

Joshua Slocum, one of the greatest sailing captains, could not find a ship to command. The world no longer seemed right for him, or so he thought as he walked the Boston waterfront. He was a man out of time, with no place to sail and no ship to captain. On a cold winter day in 1892 he met a friend along the waterfront.

"Come to Fairhaven and I'll give you a ship." The friend then paused and added, "But she'll need some repairs."

When Joshua Slocum walked into a pasture in Fairhaven, a town not far from Boston, he thought the man must have been joking. Slocum could see that the old sloop *Spray* would have to be rebuilt rib by rib, plank by plank.

Soon the word was out: Captain Joshua Slocum was in Fairhaven.

"Breaking her up?" an old man asked.

"No, going to rebuild her," Slocum answered, and set to work that very day.

He began by felling a stout oak tree for the keel. Next he rigged a steam box and pot boiler to bend the smaller trees he had cut for ribs, steaming and dressing them until they had the sea-kindly curves to support a hull across any ocean. Another oak was cut for the stem. Before the apple trees blossomed, the ribs were finished. By the time the daisies sprang up in the field, the deck was started. Soon Slocum could stand on the new deck planking and pick a handful of cherries from the tree that overhung the bow. When Joshua Slocum had finished, the *Spray* was just over thirty-six feet long and fourteen feet wide. People looked in awe at the lovely sloop that had been reborn before their very eyes. When the *Spray* was launched, Joshua Slocum wrote that "she sat on the water like a swan." Virginia had been Slocum's first love, and the *Spray* was to be his second.

# A Voyage Begins

*A thrilling pulse beat high in me. My step was*
*light on the deck in the crisp air. I felt that there*
*could be no turning back, and I was engaging in an*
*adventure the meaning of which I thoroughly understood.*

—JOSHUA SLOCUM, *Sailing Around the World*

THE MAN WHO HAD SLIPPED OUT OF TIME once again
found a place for himself. He was now determined to sail alone around
the world. No man ever had, and some said it could not be done. His
voyage started on April 24, 1895. The *Spray* made her name come true
as she sailed out across Massachusetts Bay, dashing through the waves
to catch a "necklace of spume."

From the New England coast, Slocum set his course for Nova Scotia and encountered his first big storm. He put out a sea anchor to slow the *Spray*'s speed, lashed the wheel so that she could keep a steady course, and then took short naps to catch up on his sleep. While he slept, he dreamed a whale was towing him safely through the seas. The storm eventually quieted and was followed by thick fog.

"Good evening, sir," Slocum bellowed at the man in the moon. "I'm glad to see you." The world had been wrapped in thick fog for

several days, and the waking hours could be long and lonely. Slocum worried that his voice might grow as creaky as a rusted hinge from lack of use. So he made a practice of talking to everything, starting with the moon. He also sang to the "old turtles, with large eyes, [that] poked their heads up out of the sea" and to the porpoises, who leaped at the sound of his singing. Although Slocum was sailing alone, his world became a busy one with dreams, phantoms, and conversations with the wildlife around him.

In the middle of the Atlantic, Slocum did indeed meet a friendly phantom. He had become violently ill during the height of a storm. After shortening sail by rolling it up and tying it down, he went belowdecks to sleep, for he was feeling sick to his stomach.

Something woke Slocum up, and when he looked up along the companionway from his cabin, he saw on deck a figure at the helm. It was a tall man with black whiskers, dressed in a foreign uniform from long ago. "Señor," the man said, bowing, "I am one of Columbus's crew. I am the pilot of the *Pinta,* come to aid you. Lie quiet, Señor Captain. . . . You did wrong to mix cheese with plums." Slocum had a limited amount of fresh fruits and vegetables. They were a treat on a long voyage. His food was mostly sea biscuits, salted codfish, and potatoes. "I will guide your ship tonight," said the man. And so he did. Not only then, but it seemed to Joshua that he came back many times during his long voyage around the world.

On August 4, Slocum arrived in Gibraltar twenty-nine days after he had left Nova Scotia. He planned to continue easterly through the Strait of Gibraltar into the Mediterranean Sea, but he was barely out of the strait when he saw a felucca, a ship often used by pirates, bearing down on him. It *was* pirates, and they had swept out from one of the numerous ports on the North African coast where they lurked. Slocum was no fool. He knew the odds of surviving a pirate attack were against him, and he quickly changed his plans. He would sail in a westerly direction around the world. He tacked and sailed back across the Atlantic, this time heading southwesterly toward South America and Cape Horn.

# At the Bottom of the Earth

*"Remember, Lord, my ship is small and the sea is so wide."*

—An old fisherman's prayer recited by Slocum
as he entered the Strait of Magellan

SLOCUM SAILED DOWN the east coast of South America, making many stops on the way to refit and resupply. People were fascinated by the lone sailor and were full of advice. One man gave him a large box of carpet tacks to sprinkle on deck to discourage thieves from coming aboard. The man warned him that the Fuegian people living along the Strait of Magellan near the tip of the continent were savage and every bit as dangerous as pirates.

The Strait of Magellan and Cape Horn offered the most treacherous sailing, for in this region near the bottom of the globe, the winds were the fiercest in the world. It would take Slocum two attempts to push his way through the strait, and one night at a lonely anchorage he did make good use of his carpet tacks.

Toward midnight some barefoot Fuegians tried to board the *Spray*, and Slocum was awakened by howls and felt the timbers creaking under the Fuegians' dancing feet as they jumped from the tack-covered deck directly into the sea.

On another occasion, when Fuegians in canoes tried to approach the *Spray*, Slocum fooled them by making seagoing scarecrows dressed in his clothes. He stuck them out of hatches and portholes and manipulated the figures by attached strings while he fired shots across the bows of the canoes. The Fuegians, at a distance of more than three hundred feet, thought that this was not a lone sailor, but one with a crew of cutthroats. They backed off immediately.

One evening, anchored in one of the most desolate reaches of the strait, Slocum noticed a tiny spider. It was the same size as the one that had traveled with Slocum all the way from Boston. This one he called the Fuegian spider, for it had come aboard in the strait. It began to attack the Boston spider. Slocum crouched to watch the two battle and was pleased when "my little Bostonian downed it at once," then pulled off each leg so that the Fuegian one looked more like a fly than a spider.

One day, the *Spray*'s masts became tangled in a tree's branches as she tried to leave the last cove of the strait. "Didn't you know that you couldn't climb a tree?" Slocum muttered at the *Spray*. Seven times the *Spray* had tried to sail from Port Angosto, but she was blown back each time and even caught by a tree.

Finally on April 13, 1896, she was free. Behind lay two months of fierce winds, fierce natives, and an island newly discovered by Slocum, on which he had put up a sign: KEEP OFF THE GRASS.

It was a joke, of course, for nothing grew in the desolate region at the ends of the earth. It was in this most dreary country that Slocum began to think about never again killing a living thing for food or sport. The loneliness there was so great that he "found himself in no mood to make one life less, except in self-defense."

"Hurrah for the *Spray*!" Slocum bellowed to the seals, the seagulls, the penguins, and every single creature he spotted as he finally left the strait. The little boat had seen him safely through the world's most dangerous waters, and now she was headed out across the Pacific.

# Up from the Bottom of the Earth

*All my troubles were astern; summer was ahead;*
*all the world was before me again.*
—Joshua Slocum, *Sailing Around the World*

ONCE THROUGH THE STRAIT OF MAGELLAN, Slocum headed for the Society Islands and then on to Australia. From Australia he sailed to South Africa.

After the Cape of Good Hope at the tip of Africa, the globe's other fearsome horn around which the gale-force winds roared, it was plain sailing. Heading northward now from the bottom of the world, Slocum reached Saint Helena Island. He toasted the ghost pilot of the *Pinta*, his invisible helmsman. Surely, Slocum believed, the old sailor must have assisted him in being able to find this tiny speck of land in the middle of the vast southern Atlantic.

At Saint Helena, he was given a goat to keep him company on the journey and was told the creature would be as companionable as a dog. Slocum would have loved to have had a dog aboard the *Spray*, but there was no room and he feared rabies, for which there was no cure or vaccination in those days. Slocum soon realized that the goat was the worst pirate he had ever met. It began by eating his charts, then his sea jacket, and finally his hat. He left the goat at his next stop, Ascension Island.

On May 8, 1898, the *Spray* crossed the same track she had made three years before. The little ship was truly homeward bound now. Two weeks later, Joshua Slocum doffed his cap once more to the pilot of the *Pinta* for guiding him to the island of Grenada in the eastern Caribbean. The *Spray* was "booming joyously" for home when the wind died, and she was becalmed for days on end in the Sargasso Sea. Slocum entertained himself by exploring in the great fields of seaweed for the strange animals, little and big, that swam there. He was particularly fascinated by the tiny sea horses.

A gale finally began to blow. Soon the *Spray* was "jumping like a porpoise" in the Gulf Stream as she tore her way northward again. Just off New York, a fierce electrical storm splintered the sky, and the *Spray* ran like a mad dog with bare poles, her timbers shivering and heeling on to her beam ends. But always she righted herself and sailed on.

"*Spray* ahoy!" came the call from the guard ship in
Newport Harbor. It was June 27, 1898. The harbor, a part of
Newport, Rhode Island, had been mined against the possibility
of Spanish raiders. Three months earlier, the Spanish-American
War had begun. But the sailors on the guard ship knew this little
ship and its brave captain, for people in America and around the world
had been following the voyage of the *Spray*. The sailors cheered wildly
as the sea-battered sloop entered Newport Harbor.

The *Spray* cast anchor after sailing more than 46,000 miles around
the world. Slocum had become the first person to circumnavigate the
globe alone. The voyage had taken three years, two months, and two
days, and the *Spray* was still "sound as a nut and tight as the best ship
afloat."

"If the *Spray*," Slocum wrote, "discovered no continents on her
voyage, it may be that there were no more continents to be discovered;
she did not seek new worlds . . . [but] to find one's way to lands
already discovered is a good thing. . . ."

# Epilogue

Over the next ten years, Joshua Slocum continued to journey to distant places in the *Spray*. When he was sixty-five years old, Slocum began to plan another great adventure on the *Spray*. He hoped to seek out the unknown origins of the Amazon and sail down that river to the sea. He and the *Spray* had grown old together, and this was to be their crowning voyage. As he once said, "I can patch up the *Spray*, but who can patch up Captain Slocum?"

He set sail in the autumn of 1909, but somewhere between Martha's Vineyard and his next port of call, he and the *Spray* vanished.

Joshua Slocum, like so many old Yankee seafarers, had never learned how to swim. It was his opinion that if the sea wanted him, it would come and get him.